I Am

...Just the Introduction...

Ressurrection Graves

Library of Congress Number: 2003096795
ISBN : Softcover 1-4134-3109-7

This is a work of fiction. Names, characters, places and incidents either are the
product of the author's imagination or are used fictitiously, and any resem-
blance to any actual persons, living or dead, events, or locales is entirely
coincidental.

This book was printed in the United States of America.

To order additional copies of this book, contact:
Xlibris Corporation
1-888-795-4274
www.Xlibris.com
Orders@Xlibris.com
20922-GRAV

WORLD PEACE POEM

This world was not bore
to accommodate our fleshly needs-
we have them along with free will
to accept God and Peace.

It is up to our own acknowledgement
of the depth of the need
to take the ghettos and fill them
with the living water that provides
the thick warmth of sacrificial blood
that our souls so captures and frees.

To act on the unctions that keep us breathin'-
submerge our beings
To inherit the dignity
and humility that combines,
summons powerful leaders and releases constraints
from imprisoned minds.

And we must remember the authenticity that exists when we write,
when our tongues raise to assist the function of our strong voices-
we fight!

To encourage liars to become proud of their own inhibitions
and desist from fatal convictions the truth can set us free.

We pray this nation, this world-
will make efforts to open the door out of courtesy
and open our mouths to speak

instead of being spoiled and raped by the excuses
of today's new technologies
praising the weak.

Patterns-

First to obtain our subject it must matter
with great passion-
like the most serene moment you experience-
Just you and the wind
the seconds you dance with it
at noon day with no humidity and no distractions.

Cars are honking- Passing lanes, time, lanes, Time changes, but
that moment is exposed and remembered as exquisite.

The feeling I get when I see the strong back of a man-
his movements show each morsel of definition and
I am satisfied for the day and tomorrow in my smile-

We must seek to save those lost- without Peace there is no identity,
one is incomplete- incapacitated- numb- walking, walking, walking dead and I know this to be true.

*Love and Peace are sisters, they hold hands like Chicago and
cold weather.*

I have never been there- I heard it was cold like the people
you encounter behind shopping mall counters who hate you
with their eyes-
They don't know if your life is as hateful as there's but
their bitterness thrusts the risk taking out of their bodies like
demons.

In my experience just like Poetry, Peace is coupled with wisdom,
with passion, with freedom, with order.

Nothing can be accomplished
    without Living water,
        we will forever thirst.

I mean like desert, dry cough, skeleton scaled with guck and smells
that don't wash off-

But, once you have living water it is at your disposal
to use during low times
and High praise-
It's explosive- and peace will cascade
gently with Power that leads people

to safe places inside.

Lord, let peace so reside.

Ressurrection Graves Aug. 16th, 2003

BOOK ONE

Death, Burial, and Ressurrection

CHAPTER ONE: DEATH

REAL

I don't feel sleepy although it is about time for the owls
to Whooooo!
I'm not sad because God has given me strength–
Simultaneously I stare at myself In a mirror and attempt
to script a poetic thought.

I don't feel poetically inclined I just know what I know.
What I know is loneliness as clear as the winds rage–

What I know is deep thought.
One can never deny what they feel
when it's empty inside.

Children want to know about Real, Hell,
some adults still need to know about real.

It's no jokin' matter when you have to stare at yourself
to see what optimistic attitude you can portray the fol-
lowing day so that people won't suspect your pain.

Real

You thought gangstas could harm you, no.
You're invisible compared to self mutilation without
physical wounds.

This is real.

But God has given me strength.

It's okay to be honest with what you feel,
but at least have faith that destruction will end.

With continued neglect for possible eternal damage

anybody would fall

Real.

February 11, 1998

LOCKED UP

Why are you sitting there
by the window in such a stare?

It seem to me you feel locked up,
your only wish is to be free.

You want to find happiness and go very far,
yet you feel locked up,
and can't go from where you are.

You want to take a journey across this whole land
you want no one to stop you,
but someone to hold you hand.

In many ways you feel betrayed
you feel like no one cares about who you are,
that's why you want to go very far.

This isn't easy and I know for you it's been rough,
now you feel enraged you've put your foot down
you've had enough.

Living in this world you have to be tough, to play the game,
or people will try
to run over you and you name.

This world is unfair, I know it's true;
someone always has something to say
about the way and how you do it.

If I change the world, and had power galore,
I'd command for peace love and happiness to be adorned so you
could be free of bondage, you wouldn't feel locked up no more.

October 18, 1994

BRAIN-STORM

I was sleeping last night when a pulsating—slimy—message of tissue overwhelmed the lips of my vagina—creating the illusion of this . . . this . . . It again. I've tried to let it go. A blink of an eye since it's pain. I thought I had reached a comfort zone, a remission point./

Attached to nervousness like fetus is to umbilical chord—orchestrations of operatic pitches and terrifying tones—underlying punches and crunches shielding cranium to clavicle and breastbones to waist-

In misery bleeding defeat I assume punishment and consequence for my actions—Transactions take place and cover me with blood—You heard me blood of pain—not purity.

Read a poem once—Angry at souls available to rescue her—Angry at the weak boy seeking power who committed such a hate – crime or sedu-c-tion; suction. Blinded by smiles and vibes social isms and he was cool-
I was his unprepared fool/

I read a poem about a girl vex with her insides—or was it from her insides outward she spit fueled fire and created bombs—Erupted volcanoes and dragon-flies became dragons—more capable than Mushu saving China, assassinated villains of less fortunate to class of elite, ridding the girl of her pains./

Beyond her imagination did her soul mourn-
Hatred don't make it better-

Hated until the blood from my heart tickled the walls of my inner skin- I hated until my head ached thought; aneurysm, chancing life developing immunity to clogged membranes of headaches dwelling sinus infections—Erections of mental warfare proceed my mouths confirmation. Assuming responsibility for my suppressions I plead-

Somebody Somewhere-
Soul Searchin' Please

Somebody Somewhere-
Soul Searchin' Please
Deliver Me-

I read a poem about a girl she was raped.-
I could remember descriptions of her pain as clear as the winds peace—These painful reflections reminded me—even blinded me of my therapeutic conclusions that "I have over-come" Now I write this poem—seeking refuge in its depth.

Hoping that the anger that girls poem doesn't send me back. I want to forgive. Cause if every rape victim decided to live, there'd be much stronger people, and rapists with less power. There would be a hope of a new day without the pain. There would be life where most are now chained.

Read a poem about a girl one day—She was raped like me— reminded me even blinded me of my progress—interrupted my healing process—Poem was da bomb if you're dwelling in fear— In her healing I turned back. I'm writing this poem motivated by the same spirit—Unfortunately, I have to begin again.

Read a poem about a girl one day-
I hope that girl reads mine/

Hope she finds the messages in her heart that seem hidden. It is those messages that manifest change in the spirits of victims.

Read a poem about a girl one day—inspired to transform;

I hope she reads my poem

Bouncing on the same clouds my soul believe-
I am bound as long as I'm scared to be free-
Read a poem about a girl once-
One day I'll be famous and she'll read mine.

6-5-99'

BITCHES BREW

They say position ain't got no power. White muthafucka
treat me like slaves shit.

Stupid Bitch!

Say the phone service is fucked up but I think they turned
it off and everybody is writin' complaints while Deputy's
are accepting these pleas with Big Grins and racial
outbursts.

Got men watchin' over us like Bitches in Mud, fightin'
over the scraps of our mental torture and we're bound by
walls.

Cause if I, if we, if I could be loose for a moments sake
we'd respond as we were trained, like Bitches fed raw
meat for days upon days. And this shit has got to stop
cause the devil can't make me give up.

Now I have to repent and start all over again

Between walls of storage space packed in like rats 7 females maintain as hostages creatin' a Bitches Brew!

Ressurrection Graves
September 03, 99 e99

0399

STRAY CAT

Stray Cat to my heart's content I accept the hate for I have learned thus, I cope.

Mildew on walls soggy weeds and marshmallow hope, torment of trials keeping face or atleast I try;

Black balled—Am I of separate culture standing in separate love?

Desiring my soul complete—pieces fly like a drunk in rage.

Sister soldier,
> One day you'll love me.

December 13, 1998

BLACK GIRL SLAIN

Out pouring tears wouldn't make this real-
Retaliation wouldn't change the dealer's hands-
Dealt by insanity the past be present for all the mother's.
Victims become the righteousness of God-
spirits speeding through spaces of torment/
Some make collages others make ornaments
that reflect what was seen before

BANG!
Shots fired anger forbids living-
for moments, moments of time,
we all died!

January 24, 2002
In memory of Desi

WHAT'S GOIN' ON?

Senseless acts of violence Painful-
I saw him that night surround sound-
Whispers of . . . Melodies of . . . Re-
    flections of . . .
I saw him that night . . .

He bounced that ball He sang that tune
He danced that night to the sounds of
    delusion-
He screamed that night Take em' to da
    whole-
His imaginary friend
If the walls could tell of his visions
    his thought-
What is it that has consumed every
    thought,every touch—his spirit-
In the pit of my stomach the acid is
deactivated by a drowning water fall of
    tears-held within-
My heart building it's ark to avoid de-
    struction
blood vessels and collapsed muscles
I am embraced by the consumption of pain-
I saw him dancing—I saw his moves-
Baddest man on the floor—In his mind he
    was the baddest man on the court.
As the music played and our souls began
    to soar to the melody and harmony of
    rhythms—He made the winning basket-
Yeah, the championship game-
Senseless acts of violence-
Young brotha gave him more-
More venom to fight off the tangibles of
    life-
more poison to flea the possibility of
    progress
Senseless acts of violence-
You don't hear about that on Television-
        Marvin said it best—"What's goin'
    on?"

Ressurrection Graves
4-29-1999

Home Going Celebration Of
Jason Gregory Owens

December 18, 1980 ~ May 3, 2003

Tuesday, May 13, 2003
Viewing: 10:00am   Service: 11:00am

Rhema Christian Center Church
1825 Michigan Avenue, NE   *Washington, DC 20018*

Bishop Clarence C. Givens
Officiating Minister

"Precious in the sight of the Lord is the death of His saints."
Psalm 116:15

ROCK BOTTOM

We are at War!

Live by da . . . . . (Gun)   Die by da . . . . (Gun)

How many brothas fell victim to da streets, rest in peace young nigga
there's a heaven for a G . . .

We are at War;
War when our "G's" believe that freedom is after death and their
present state of living is not going to effect their destination.

People wanna know how I'm coping-
I don't know and it's just of personal interest, It's fam-
It's like a long distance friendship.
My heart just says Damn.

Live by da . . . Die by da . . .

Murder was the case that they gave me.

Yeah, I'd like to pour out liquor for my homey on lock down, 6 feet
under and all my homies watching over me/

We live our lives in the rhythm of
gangsta beats left after

bullet shells hit
highly concentrated streets;

Rock Bottom

It's hard knocks for those who choose to dodge em'-
bullets; skulls shattered- left in fragments an ohm of sadness./

Many find gladness in the beef.-
It's like a sickening disease./
Many chief like it's crack-
fact is there is no ease on disaster;
           Contact./

He's in the waiting room
praying that we know,
he's proud and he loves us so.

Live by da … Die by da …
My eyes left white when
moments turn between existence and non-
and fear of the news left visions of us
gathered together to mourn.-

It was like the moment between
seeing the child in the crosswalk,
tires screeching, and a car horn/
I saw lights.

In the flesh, we play God
of the pavement-
Injuries; Enslavement
to a master not our own/

Front Line—we stand on
to sense the next attack.
We do things
that only God could bring back./

We mourn, but somebody
will be born again (today I believe),
even if it takes another body bag
and a flag drenched in blood
to be risen-

For third eyes to influence weak systems
about God-bodied decisions/

Even if the blood drops into the soil of demons
to make Christ like beings out of the toughest heathens/
    I believe,
and you can count that on my breathin/

you'll get it—Admit it. Submerge you entire soul in it.
Why wait for another body to be laid to rest./

I see these streets never changing. They will always exist.

But do you really want to be a part of this?

And, if everything were Perfect,
there would be no balance,
but you don't have to worship violence.

Some of y'all get it, and some of you won't,
because the thrill of being evil is much easier
than to address the baggage some of you tote./

Many of you find it hard to feel emote-
Please—Giving change a subtle thought,
you find leads everyday
to possess new levels of ought.

It's life that you are numb to-
I've been there,
it's cold and unfruitful-
paranoid that everybody will use you./

Live by da … Die be da …
Murder was the case that they gave me ….

But God saved me/

I hit my rock bottom
and it was all I needed to change direction.
Take that fake S off yo' chest/
Let Jason's legacy be a form of a resurrection
for the living in death.

You can choose your rock bottom to be last Saturday morning
or whenever you heard,
or you can wait til I get a call
to write a poem at yo' funeral-

Somebody say
WORD!

May 10, 2003
TO: Jason and the Jefferson family and friends.

RAPE

Nobody knows . . . .
Old people, young people, we now fight to determine
who's seen more,
who's been hurt or affected by more
and it's the advocate for deeper suppression;
a mouth piece for confession
and compassionate eyes to glow, grow, glow.
Who's been raped more me or you?
To me, that's to broad a question. And how many times
have you raped yourself, screaming orgasms that you
don't enjoy because you're too busy trying to figure
out whether he'll call you tomorrow—now that's sor-
row
Like torn tears—inviting friends over to sooth your
rivers with waterfalls of Kirk Franklin.
I know that I can make it . . . . .
Knowing you'll walk around fakin' it, until you cry
again. See, you broke down your damn and overflow
with raving waters
that make you
a walking
wet dream./

Ressurrection Graves
November 2000

AT THE EDGE

I am challenging my reality by standing at the edge
I am standing at my challenges facing the reality of overboard.
I am challenging my stand of who's purpose to reveal,
I am standing at the challenge of my realities to overcome its disap-
    pointments.
I am at the edge of my existence, which provides a reality unashamed,
because my realities feel so challenged by numbness that I have lost
touch with my life.

        I am at the center of self and still—moments have lapsed time
for me.
I am at the center of self where my edge communes.
It is tough to take a mirror and see reality.

I am standing at the edge of my numbness, praying for feeling again,
that I might challenge my capacity to be imperfect: to be human.

I am standing with myself to address my inflictions,
I am standing here to challenge death with my awakening!

An attempt to fly from the edge, renew my youth and increase my
wisdom.
Fearlessly fly and have faith that the wind is God's breath assuming
position.

And I am challenging Satan to free me of his plans, but, because of
my God, it would cost too much if I jump over and he let me land:
                Above him
                without a fight.

I am challenging my realities and the forces that hinder my perfec-
tion.
I am challenging my fears that hinder the very instep of my election.

I am challenging the faith that I have which is more than my condition.
I am leaning on the cornerstone where the edge is a victim.
and with all of the knowledge, I still manage to obstruct the vision.

I am standing and I am feeling the wrath of my tampering,
and at the edge, I attempt to end my inquisitions with fate.

Is fate capable of pressure?
Does it manipulate with selected pathways?
If I go slow or fast lane, right or left?
Does fate change with your odyssey?
     I say yes,
but if I jump from the edge will I fly,
     or kill myself?

March 12, 2002

THE TRUTH IN LIES

You never tell the truth, no matter what you're going through.
You always seem to lie and I know there's a reason why.
You feel your face has to change, in order to deal with me.
Is that really freedom, completion with self,
I'm not concerned about me or us, more than how are you really inside.
Why do you feel the need to lie?
Is that really freedom completion with self?/

It's often times that we find ourselves changing to please others-happiness becomes irrelevant and it becomes this great excuse to avoid consequence/
When I die- Somebody better know me./ If I live life lying to avoid confrontation, and make everybody else feel like linen- when will my satin skin reach it's beginning, in truth/
I stand to question righteousness but, not of you, or you, of myself and- if someone happens to point out a weakness-
I am strong enough to take it and change according to the God that wills me- do you feel me/
I can't lie to you because you might get mad- I'm glad that by me telling the truth that is my contribution to you learning me-whether my voice or reasoning is acceptable to you has nothing to do with me- you take what I give and choose your response, it then becomes your stuff not mine. Don't have expectations of me/
By telling the truth, I reach to embrace learning, discerning the information that is given and I find new ways to be a virtuous woman. If I can't cook I want to learn before I get a husband, I am not going lie and say I can burn when, I can really burn down your house.
I'm not going tell some unnecessary man that I am pregnant to keep him- if he leaves, he wasn't mine y'all. I don't want nothing that is not for me. I am not going to tell my girlfriend that I can't hang out with her because I have writing to do when I really just

don't want her company. I am going to figure out why I don't want her company and communicate to her why it is that I don't want her company. If it is true friendship, honesty will not break us up.

And when I die I refuse for people to stand up proud say that I was this great inventor- of stories- lies that were creative, but, nobody could vouch for knowing me. In fact, they began to lie to fill up the time between the choir singing and the reading of the obituary.

Please, I want one person to talk about my work, somebody to talk about my love for God, another to talk about love, my love for everything that moved me, and I want folks to party most of all. I want people to be happy because they know where I came from, where I was at, and dance like David because they knew where I was going. I want folks to discuss there most precious times with me and remember my legacy in that way.

Most of y'all, are wigglin' in yo' seats because I am discussing death. If that's what you got, you missed the topic. Lying is abusive and self destructive. You only lie to yourself whether the person knows that you are lying or not. It's like a strong drug. To remain on top, you must keep feeding yourself. Often times people lie so much that they lose their own identity in it. It's also like an addict in the sense that we try to make everything legal or illegal or say that a little white lie is smaller than a big white one. Lies are lies yall and only truth can change that.- Keep it real/ only you know if it is and rock on/

August 11, 2001

CHAPTER TWO: BURIAL

LORD I PRAY

Sometimes you want to run,
but you can't go anywhere.

Like a foot stuck in cement,
you can't leave from there.

The pain exhausts you,
as overwhelming as it may seem,
bewilderment invites itself in your mind,
anger and rage fulfill your dream.

This world, lost without direction.
Needing desperately guidance and protection.

Our foundation, our home
is here and **WILL STAY**
and in our prayers we shall say:

Father, I am yours,
young, strong and bold.
Through you I work to show,
life's treasure's unfold.

So much work,
and time is running out.
Show me Lord, you way,
dispel every doubt.

FAITH, FAITH, and **LOVE** we need,
in order to restore,
our lost generation indeed.

So help us Lord,
those willing and confused,
those in pain and those abused.

Bring us all,
teach us your special way.
Protect us and guide us,
as we walk your path each day.

Temptation and fear
is below us now,
Saints he is here,
THE DEVIL IS GOIN' DOWN!!!

Lord for those
who do not know the way,
use me, guide us, protect us all Lord.
In Jesus name I pray,

And the church shouts:

AMEN

3-18-97

WHITE NIGGA

If I run, will you run after me?
These woods clean as Mama's home-
    trees bare and dead; air as cold as a baby still born.
If I run will you shoot me in the distance, and use me as a trophy? If I
run, will you let me free?

I know you heart,
unlike the cares of most like you-
because you love for m,
    you a nigga too.
"White Nigga 's what they'd call you."

If I run will you tell?
I'm just one nigga gon' They won't know-
    Will you conscious be ruled by your race or your soul?

Your people who accept you
only because of your face or your God?

"White Nigga," you my folks, because you care. Yo' conscious over-
whelms your desire to keep me.
    "Nigga to Nigga", If I run, will I live?

Ressurrection Graves
January 10, 1999

MY ROOM

People here, people there
Why do people always stare?

They want to know me to get inside my brain,
I wish someone else could feel my pain.

They want me to come out
to get inside my heart,
They want to know what I'm about
wondering, what takes her heart apart.

My room is this special place
where no one can intrude,
the walls are all white, and
I have my own space
where no one can be rude.

In my room, I can scream aloud
and no one can hear me.
In my room, I can cry aloud
and let my feelings run free.

In my room, my imagination takes control,
my dreams become real in my heart and in my soul.

My room contains one window
in which I look and dreams are true.
I gaze at the stars and tell 'em all my dreams,
then they become real to me just like you.

So, in my room I dream, I cry, I scream, I die.

To the world I am dead because I go into my room often,

I will probably stay there until

peace makes the hearts of men soften.

July 21, 1996

DEVEN

He did it, it ended
and the pain
was left behind-

our selfishness came out in tears,
our praises went upstairs with him-
in his arms-
carried the whole of everybody to the ark
and our spirits marched together there.

Danced with Jesus in Glory
and was apart of his welcome home celebration-

we stand captivated at the strength
and the faith that filled this room-

the tongues that went out-
the people that moved from stillness-
cold and lonely places-
spaces take time like constants-
and life exists forever among those who believe-
Thank God for freedom, Deven rests in Peace!

August 2001
"Deven I love you, thank you for sharing your life with us"

I APOLOGIZE

For . . . All the times I had sex without your blessing.
        For the times I did not pray to simply please you, and thank you.
For the times allowed the music to fantasize me into an infatuation.
For the poison I endured, do to disobedience/
For all of the shameful sins and the one's that I possess secretly.
For the times I cried worry instead of praising you-
you inhabit the praises of your people/

For the situations that forced me to hear you.
For the walks late at night to find you.
You were there all the time-
You were present like the most precious
of all that could've been received
and when he hurt me; and ,
sex became a vicarious action to reach oneness-
I thank you for loving me anyway/

You stood for me-
You bled for me/
made my wounds yours-
you fixed if Lord/

I was empty and I did not want to kill myself because I was already dead.

I died at 12.

For all the times I thought, I was right and I was not.
For everything that I made love to,
became head over heels with
and you did not come first.

I want to say that I am sorry–

I clench this word and now use it for cleaning,
healing and allow this process to run its course–
In case I bleed I do, For the expense
that I find you, in that blood/ same veins;
I love you and, for all of the lust, the impatience,
the pregnancy scares, my fears, diseases, sicknesses–

For every moment I tried to run up the steps
but my legs were not strong enough to walk yet,
For all the things that would and could destroy me.–

I love you and I apologize./
For my rebellion—for my rapes—for my excuses/
For fornication, the blood you shed for me that I abused.

For the things I tried, to escape.
For the times I did not keep my house clean,
for the times that I was not clean—inside/
I love you, and I apologize.

Ready; eternally

For the times I ignored your fire lighting the sky
        I apologize.
Forever—for everything I do as a thing that is not of you–

I apologize. Thank you for giving me—Love, in spite of the tears

you may have cried cause of me,

I cry painfully,
        I apologize.

July 28, 2001

I MUST CONFESS

I, I have these thoughts that many are terrified to admit.
And, even in this season, this year—it is still so difficult to handle it.
I am speaking of these thoughts that invade the very private parts in my
    head.
These thoughts, make me afraid of my destiny. God has vested so much
    in me.
And I try to understand why some folk don't feel attached to legacy and
    truth—to the foundation that has been laid—with purpose to aid
    and counsel the paths I choose.

Even without words.

I have fantasies that if played out could change my life—I'd be a living
    hypocrite and I would not be committed to the one: Christ.

And it scares me!

I don't know what to do with it.
My thoughts they go on and I become consumed in it.
I know that "feelings keep us feinin'" and the spiritual realm is where we
    should lie.

It scares me that I feel like I want to live in this state of mind.
Christians would say "it's the trick of the enemy" and I believe it's true
    because this change would be a life commitment not a sin that you
    repent from and become new.

I am broken—imagining what I would say if my daughter came home
    this way—What would she say if I came home this way. Looking for
    an excuse to suit my situation—I think of the one's I have heard
that some people's lives are engraved in-

"I was born this way", "Pain made me change", "It was always there, I give

you my word."

I know that demons don't travel alone and they flow in relatives. Abuse carries fornication, homosexuality, and other demons like such for example.

I keep claiming deliverance but the devil won't leave me alone he keeps clampin' on to my wounds and pretends to sooth but he's really just working his way in to consume my peace with his craftiest tools. I am attempting to expose my demons so they don't feel like they can weaken me with manipulation and fear. I don't wanna be here.
I notice that I am attracted to those I innocently want to protect and love and who remind me of me—but something, (I'll leave without description) I'm practicing celibacy cause I need to figure this out. And it seems I am more attacked when I am by myself.

And, most folk are fearful of being alone—only God knows.
I love him and when the holy spirit is in—I feel it—and when I get to praying I mean it and when something's about to go down I discern it. God prepares me for big things so I can be available to help others grieve.

I am afraid that my life change will not be my destiny designed for me but the destiny I've chosen.

Now I see from a lot of their eyes—we just wanna be loved. I know I owe em'.
My position: I can be happy in both situations, to be honest.
I won't be holy though. I can feel ecstasy in both situations. The spirit of it is suspect though. I won't feel connected to Christ quite the same—I may miss a revelation I may blaspheme his name,
And the Lamb's book of life is where my name is to be written. I am afraid of rewriting the vision.-
I am convinced I was given a place here to lead—led by God.
I have been fighting for my identity since I can remember.
God has given me one and now fear kindles. My thoughts take me

somewhere else. My heart is aching so bad—no one knows.

Thing is, when I am in the spirit, I feel differently about it all. Everyone is
so concerned with now and they say, "Live to the fullest".
The thoughts and beliefs are all cerebral and justified.
I just keep thinking of my eternal home. That is what truly matters.
So why can't I get rid of the demons that try to encourage me to change.-

They do flee when I say Jesus, Jesus, Jesus's name that's why I know it's
official.
There are lifestyles we choose.
Gangstas homosexuality Promiscuity False Preaching and hundreds
more I could add to the list.

I am afraid I may have won some of those battles but, what if I can't win
the war.

My mate would have to be as close to Christ as incredible can get for
me, because just like God saves me—through prayer my partner
will be a savior in a sense truly supplied to me by God's awesomeness. It hurts to think I may not make it in—and thanks to God this
is my decision.
I don't know who this is supposed to help but I can't keep it private—I'd be
holding a lie in-

I know he wants me—Satan is a bad man supernatural that is but God is
the author and his omnipresence puts Satan in straight fear, I don't
have an answer now for where I stand—I'd just hate to be held in this
box of sorts like DC streets—if you don't get a taste of other places
you'll be stuck here and you may not recognize open doors.

So I thank God for my mother how she prayed for me when I saw other
people's mama's high off crack and they were catching their mamas
giving head in the living room at 4 am to random crack head cats.

And I thank God for the things I experienced cause I was a different

child I wasn't like the rest. Yeah, I was in the streets but at 2 am you could also find me either at a bus stop or a park, laying on a bench looking at the stars talking to God or on the basketball court; shooting the ball with no lights for 2 reasons, so predators wouldn't see me if I had to run, and so my shot would be radar hoping to play next season.

The truth is, everybody's afraid of everybody's "stuff", cause they just don't want anymore, and nobody knows how to handle exposure believers and non–

Again we must be born.

And I don't know the outcome of my confession but I know my closet is empty and my heart must go on—so like the fighter I am. I'll do it even if I stand alone.

Our iniquities are not normal even if everybody does it, and they must be addressed.
It doesn't mean tomorrow I'll be perfect and before I become more redundant—I hope you pray for me—I hope you see my intentions are to be freed from bondage.

And there is one thing I have learned; just because you ask to be saved, ask to be delivered, ask to be forgiven don't mean you do it one time it's the difference between having a child and being its parent—adoption

The difference between loving to write, and cultivating the gift.

The difference between being bold enough to expose yourself until healing begins, and living begins, and sin ends … maybe not all … but the process of it all makes you so much more whole.

And I don't know if I'll ever write a poem again, I hope so …
I don't know if this changed anyone's life—but, I'm gonna meditate on

this day and night, until I get it, until I receive it cause I need to until the need for understanding is clear.

Until God shows me how to overcome this , I will press.

Our iniquities are not normal even if everybody does it, and they must be addressed.
It doesn't mean tomorrow I'll be perfect and before I become more re-dundant—I hope you pray for me—I hope you see my intentions are to be freed from bondage.

And there is one thing I have learned; just because you ask to be saved, ask to be delivered, ask to be forgiven don't mean you do it one time it's the difference between having a child and being its parent—adoption

The difference between loving to write, and cultivating the gift.

The difference between being bold enough to expose yourself until healing begins, and living begins, and sin ends . . . maybe not all . . . but the process of it all makes you so much more whole.

And I don't know if I'll ever write a poem again, I hope so . . .
I don't know if this changed anyone's life—but, I'm gonna meditate on this day and night, until I get it, until I receive it cause I need to until the need for understanding is clear.

Until God shows me how to overcome this , I will press.

Our iniquities aren't normal even if everybody does it, and they need to be addressed
So here I go, Lord I love you and so this, my sins, I must confess.

June 5, 2003

CHAPTER THREE: RESSURRECTION

MOVE WITH THE CLOUDS

We shall dance with clenched hands-
Nurtured in the bosom of the spirit/
Campfires upon campfires
tribal unity amongst all Indians-
congregations will sing in harmony of
greatness and peace./
All races will hold one thread of the
    garment
That this great creator is standing in—
    all singing to his
Glory in grace for his mercy and power-
Singing in 100's of languages—those who
    can not sing
will be driven to lead with angelic hymns/
It will be like fire—like floods and all
    the people will have touched this gar-
    ment-
And all will stand/ In hundreds of lan-
    guages we will sing
"Move with the clouds"
Whirlwinds will rush in and collect all
    of the pain and hate and torment-
All will submit to the glory of the
    Lord—some will fall short of his glory,
Others will stand-
How great is that!

April 02–1999

CALL IT ... POETRY

Even if it seems hard, the ink that is, write until the pen loses focus then let it spill into 3D, spoil it with songs and let it's lyrics breathe/ Uniquely explain the thoughts that enter-tame you—call it poetry— call it spoken word—call it, call it call it what it must hear to regurgitate the oxygen you've birthed in it/ they call that air-
Somewhere nigh along the banks of your
paps lye babies that foresee just like Jesus but remain sovereign internally to be filled with the holy ghost running like rivers to find their own stars; climb the walls of rightful men to call it righteousness in the hearts of them/ with sweet waters glistenin' we melted our castles in the sand made brown sugar/ Reformed the trees—just to lie them down and put our initials inscribed—Forever soaked, I execute myself to channel the antennas, died in saturation of sinner's blood—caught umbilical chords choking me with threats of dismissal from human coves—I told death that I was robed in flesh—sold and blessed/ the exterior stands—I oath insemination—loathed in a craft man's plan/

Early December 2000

ORGASM

YOU'VE BROUGHT ME TO A PLACE
I'VE KNOWN—
TO EXIST SOMEWHERE
LIKE MOTHERLESS CHILDREN—
MY HEART RAN SCARED—
I WAS UNPREPARED FOR WHAT
WAS IN STORE/
AND IT WAS MUCH, MUCH MORE/

December 28, 2000

Much more like til' death do us part and meet forever walking streets of gold and fruits that nourish the soul/ serving you by way of eternal bliss. People complain about the risks, the things that are given up to serve— those things that don't help you become better—you purge. Purge as you've never. Don't just touch the water be baptized in it. Invite the people to come light incense and spit lyrics as your old man is descended. Hip hop has many parts—I carry the flavor of it. Juices erect the information that centers me from the spirit I am an artist listed in the great book I meet spoken word at the heart. Hearts contain the thump/ I quote lyrics many of you will masturbate because of it/ not me—the illusion of the orgasm brings you pleasure—just breathe/ the inhalation of the father himself makes my feet move to the rhythm of David/ I have become this willing vessel for two—words spoken to sound and God's glory submerged into my being/ Yes I got a testimony—I got more than just one—I could fall under the power of the holy ghost while I am rhyming in the shower or singing originals at Barnun/ see I don't take this meeting that we experience and leave without change—someone is in search of change right now, that same someone may search their whole lives, CHANGE for me is not to leave the same.

I'm not goin' miss my blessing so If you searching for this supreme orgasm and it hasn't touched you yet, You are searching in pussy holes and phallic symbols of the microphone/ you may be peeking in corners of the earth to find nature and through making love to it—the desire is to make it love you. / You have these desires to attain an ultimate something, but, deny your spirit to move to it—trying too hard to understand your spirit that you don't allow it lead—you want to know the palpitations by which it breathes-

For all things aren't given at once to teach how to sustain/ through peace do we learn the things that will cause what is change/ (And God does not violate your will)—And what he's done for me may not be your same deliverance and the things that he's shown me may not be your prophetic images but/ if we could just shut—up long enough to discern—he would teach us to weed out the things that weren't given for learning and shield us from things that would later hurt/ and he would make the things we most desire everlasting—fasting with prayer and through supplication we rise—I make application to the information that he has made through word—confirmed by my third eye and eye can't imagine the life that I used to live compared to this one/ Orgasms are physical of what we would love to attribute to complete spirit—some of yall mad because I am speaking truth—can't have orgasms because It would take too much out of you and you scared—I would be afraid to bare my soul to someone who I knew did not really love me too/ so why you keep letting the devil make love to you./
And this joy I have can't get any higher I used to say but—he takes me to higher heights and teaches me new ways to influence and inform/ new ways that he makes ruin of my mistakes and gives me light to shine—I rock on/ I rock on and thank him for stepping up to the mic—be-coming my peace and letting me be used for his might/ No orgasm I have ever experienced could ever move me like this—people ponder my executions but it's really as simple as—in order to obtain fruitful, everlasting bliss I must be submerged into the existence of the one who brought me out of death-

I place peace to the scene and receive like boomerangs so the Black Women could greet each other/ I want that woman to know that I isn't about bangin' that brotha/ Get out cho' feelins'

And, I love my own behind I don't want yours—wanna concentrate on things like excellency and if you are made whole or otherwise important by grittin' on me—Then, you can't ever complain about statistics my Nubian, Bohemian, "Righteous", sista/ Say "hi," It's just a salutation, not long walks through cold winters/

In order to exercise Free—and politically rest as a part of what is revolution—

Please take your pollution and examine it—and touch orgasm/ put your hands in it/ Please without judgment, allow the mirror to tell you the truth/ I love you—regardless/ and far; flesh is carnal and orgasms increase, not with people—but with you—Peace/

July 28, 2001

DESI

It would be much too easy for me
to mourn and weep–
You are free and
have a sleep that is eternal.

Inspiration lies in the smile you'd give,
when we sang "For you I will".

I will pour out water from tear-ducks,
so fears will get dealt wit.

I felt it so deeply, walked on rivers that
graced me wit reflections of you in a crowd;
shouting for Jesus to come down,
so our souls would share worship.

Yes our Lord is
calling for a people who
love him to lead–
by his blood we are freed–

Mommy in sacrifice, he chose me.
        The greater reward is the latter.
Nothing on earth can bling like his rings of righteousness
        that would bring joy to darkness so that light can come in.
And, many of you mourn. Hearts torn with uncertainty and pain./

CRY, CRY, CRY until the tears themselves
can build the strength to walk away
and become new again.
Let out your pain with cheers of praise,
raise a standard against all odds.–
'cause the devil, he can't woop God.

And I, I stand between spaces—faceless now.
Just tasteless but, there is food for miles.—I'm okay-
By grace, I'm saved.
And someday you'll know, that in heaven I await you.

I am resting that you too, will come.

I may be 5, but this situation is bigger
than the circumstance and the reasons.

It is time for a new season!

For folks who believe to put faith to their beliefs and . . .

For people to understand what love is
before words exchange, in all kinds of relationships.

I am not here because
my purpose is fulfilled,
to bring you together.
You've been given free will but,
you determine whether you serve God or man.

I love you all, I am definitely doing well up here,
and if it be true, that I, Desi was a part of helping change,

Then, I would die again and again for God.
That's love unconditional. I love you Ma.

January 26, 2002

LIBERTY

Do you ever think that your present condition,
regardless of what it is in terms of pleasure, is death?

Can we as humans walk dead?

It is our spirit that is dead and many of us are unaware
that one could be dead or alive.

We are comfortable in our iniquities
because we are not free of want, and free of need.

We believe that freedom is to want,
to need and to fulfill thereof.

We do not see our weakness until it has gone,
or tortured our souls to interior mourning.

Free to some, is bondage.

And our escape is not priority often
because the bondage sustains our sight.

And, our habits are conditioned by the
fabrications we tell our self to fall further from grace.

And death is living, and death is breathing
and death is freedom to some.

> But death is carnal.
>   It is not eternal.
>   It is not freedom.
>   It seems fun.

Death is not amusing.
Death is a great imitator of life.
As Satan is a Great imitator of God.
But, he can't win.
He can't win.

As you, I have been given free will.
Death is my choice.
Life is my choice.

In school, if you followed any child,
did you follow the follower, or the leader?

The leader prepared you to lead.

The follower imitates the Leader,
but always falls short of victory
because his power is limited, to imitation.

Death is not death to the living
because death imitates,
it could never live.

Once death has manifested,
only the Leader,
the creator can resurrect the dead.

Death has sight. Life has vision.

If I abstain from want, I can not covet.
If I do not need, my belly will be fat;
my shelter secure; my peace embodied.

Free of desire is to be strong in spirit.

And death can not have me,

because needs, desires, and this world,
I abandoned when I began living in freedom.
I do not encounter darkness,
        I have Liberty.
        I am Light.

March 21, 2002

I AM RESSURRECTION

I am Ressurrection, not the Resurrection, the Resurrector—just me.
I come without form or fashion just absent from the body to exchange pain, with Joy. Some can't get used to the new name cause
they think they know me—That blows me/Ressurrection is everything that I have ever been in God's calculated form—forgiven—and
risen—I come back from the graves-
Just to keep the microphone warm—for you/
I stand before you nakedly and risk being called anything—less than—
not worthy of/
I ain't here to pretend to be prophetic—I am graced—blessed with
holy boldness and I stand clearly in his image—like I would Michael
Jordan at a Wizards scrimmage—Blemished,
Blemished and torn where my life had broken standards and boundaries were not set so I increased my failures—and you wonder why he
gave me—Ressurrection the Spiritual Soul-Ja.
I can make lists of times that I was not acting like a Christian—But,
that is why I am forgiven. Your love might help me see evidence of the
son in sweet rotation—help me make differences where my boundaries exist risk taken—God is so patient—Days numbered like I notice when rays of the son seem missing—some days I just thank him
because I am living-
Everybody relates to pain—I want an audience who can relate to
change—Forget the marketing and the rented Bentley to impress
you—I came in my Suzuki Esteem to testify that my God reigns and
loves you no matter what you do./
I stand nakedly and give. I stand here as I am and live/ As for mistakes
all of us have them, if mine don't make sense to you—then maybe you
don't have to understand them/ But you could pray for me—and like
Sheba the Queen, that would be alright with me.
I Stand lifted, gifted in a zone that propels the inner meaning of me.
I change daily to encompass new standings. Created I to diminish the
possibility of never advancing.

People put a place on poetry, but it's possible that as music saves,
often with the beat, lives can be changed with the acapella version,
lyrics in heat like fire—I rock the entire situation wit clear vision-
Never distorted, always committed/
to the microphone—feelin' like, the holy ghost when I spit it—take it in
before I deliver—always pregnant to birth new rivers of life—born to
confiscate the mic—
Laced words wit the depth and height of Christ/
Applauding me—I outta be able to close my mouth and still have the
words come out/
like my CD blowout/ Sale—Look out—at the nearest-
I got finger tips that tingle when the masterpiece is speaking to my
spirit-
Got God on the inside blessin' the lyric like Aunt Jemama is to
syrup/
Bottom line, my part is to deliver it the way he gives it-
linen in the winds be the fabric of our lives-that—move the words
between spaces—makes doves fly—Together
and Ressurrection has weathered storms—all while God kept me
warm in his word—Ver-ba-tum I apply it to safe stages like—my
shower—praise him for hours/ water sort of had me frozen when I
finished-
I have been chosen wit lips scented; frankincense did it-
had you paralyzed from the waste down-
cause I am intoxicating from the inside and on the way out/
Stronger than coffee black I attack situations with forces
distort your fond memories with light exposure/ Spiritual Soul-Ja
present to hold it down—inspite of the haters I will advance from
stagnate grounds/ Ignition of the pen to cum all over the paper, left
the after party of the performance so you can soak it in later/
Fans don't make you friends and love of my work don't make you love
me—it just enhances the possibilities/
Just like Fossils and fertility—we invest in subjects that develop from
the id—We consume the information like inhaling Jamaican Weed
and hope that the hypothesis is promising—hope it has no flaws-\
our mistakes lie when we exclude God.

You are dismissed/ channel this, like MTV's new guide to ruin self-esteem—but, it's National?
Names kept enclosed like sacred message bottles/
I want to sound cute like Nelly Furtado wit the power of Jamal St. John-
I rip it wide open wit the gloves or the mic on.
I stand on top of disasters, like morning afters/
I flow to the extent that I am required to get the applause that make God himself pass out freedom fliers; miles at a time/
I elevate from my adolescence to the woman I am—been struggling not to throw the hands—cause it's just easier sometimes-
we rely on the methods that require little thought—so in situations now I pray stronger—so not to offend anyone's face with my fist—heavy like ten forklifts-
Been strugglin' not to make my intimate battles scripted on poetic lines-
but, somebody somewhere will take the time to heal from domestic violence—like I am trying to, and somebody's man might wipe the tears from her eyes with us-
Enough to listen to her heart beat through – through it/
I see the vision of me on Oprah Winfrey—trying to be the Youngest among the Heavy weight Poet's—shout out

I am Ressurrection, not the Resurrection, the Resurrector—just me.
I come without form or fashion just absent from the body to exchange pain, with Joy. Some can't get used to the new name cause they think they know me—That blows me/Ressurrection is everything that I have ever been in God's calculated form—forgiven—and risen—I come back from the graves-
Just to keep the microphone warm—for you/

For real—I just want what God has in store, I owe it to him—for the incredible distribution of grace-
On time—never ceasing to infiltrate the situation and make improvements/ handle all my loose ends/

I am Ressurrection, not the Resurrection, the Resurrector—just me.
I come without form or fashion just absent from the body to exchange pain, with Joy. Some can't get used to the new name cause
they think they know me—That blows me/Ressurrection is everything that I have ever been in God's calculated form—forgiven—and
risen—I come back from the graves-
Just to keep the microphone warm—for you/

End of 2002/Beginning 2003

BOOK TWO

Eros vs. Phileo

CHAPTER ONE: FRIENDSHIP

SOUL JOYS

Through the moons and the rivers
flow a peace like the center of your eyes.

I am isolated as I reflect thoughts of you.
It is deep like ocean view daydreams that go for miles and miles . . . .

Without you, my mind is weary
and my body is cold.
Like a newborn separated from its mothers wound.
It's like a diva without soul–
It's meaningless and insignificant.

The stars speak to my heart,
and embrace my love without condition.

The breeze of soft spoken wind feels my pain
and encourages my tears, for healing.

Moment like these the depth of a place
by which I was unaware existed.

In That moment . . . . . .
A hymn of love, of pain, of worship, of faith, of courage,
and defeat all crept into the walls of my soul.

My wounds began to mend,
from abuse and torment.
I was touched by a joy that made my spirit fly–
like a colored child running through a cornfield–

My soul embraced that love
That no words could define.

And then, in my sweet somber.
I could see the Southern Baptist Church in Alabama humming
the same hymn in Heaven. I could feel the short breathes of air
from the thin fan that was given out every Sunday. I could see
the pain hidden in their unconditional faith.
I could see God's favor flowing through those who live to worship
him.

Peace like a river–
the chains are broken.
Peace like a river–
The battle is won.
Peace like a river–
The war has just begun.
And on that day when all is said and done
and my imagination is no longer my mercy.
And on that day when flesh no more,
I will embrace heaven as I do every moment
I feel peace like a river.

September 25, 98

LOVE IN A YEAR'S TIME

I woke up this morning with an unusual smile,
I had a feeling I hadn't felt in a while.

A sense of relaxation and happiness came over me,
my spirit was lifted and my heart, set free.

The birds were humming and the sun was bright,
the trees slightly blowing and it felt so right.

I felt secure and loved and ecstatic inside,
I'm sure this feeling was real this feeling I could not hide.

The day went on my feelings never changed . . .
weeks went by, my heart felt the same.

A year has gone by and throughout the hard times,
I've figured the happiness may stem from the fact that you are
mine.

From the first day I woke up with a new driven smile,
until tonight when I rest and pray for our child,
this happiness and relaxation comes from only one thing,
I'm in love and it makes my heart sing.

It took a while for me to grasp
that I could share love and it would last.
I would do anything for this love to remain,
because this feeling wasn't here before you came.

As I lay down tonight dreaming of you,
I'm praying that I wake up and this poem sustains its truth.

This day is over so I'll close my eyes,

thanking God for this love in a Year's time.
I love you Always!

January 25, 1996

MY CHILD

My child as you lay in your bed,
listen to my voice and the stories I've read.

I watch you sleep
you're a part of me.
I give you love
to set you free.

As you rest your eyes
understand what I say and
Angels will watch over you
to make sure you're okay.

Don't be afraid
you have nothing to fear.
Sleep well my child
knowing that God is near.

Give love to receive
always have faith and believe
God will get you though
because his love is unconditional and true.

My child how innocent you are
know that your mother is never far.

Little child close you eyes
mommy's here so don't you cry.

I love you now and forever
when you awake in the morning
we'll be together.

So close your eyes and
let God observe you   to prevent all harm,
he'll see you through.

Give love to receive
always have faith and believe,
God will see you though
because his love is   unconditional and true.

March 5, 1996

I AM PROUD TO LOVE

I am Proud to love.
I have known you for a time.
I have known you in an intimate, sensuous fashion.
My silky overlap has quivered to the swaying
Of your tongue messaging me with your motions.
My soul has slept on your ability to make me yearn.
Yearn for more in a loving intangible love, surpassing
    all fleshly desires.
I am Proud to have loved you.
I am softened by the embrace of love-
I am melting at the sight of you-
I am becoming a spirit in the midst of breeze that has
    swept me inside of you.
I am touching you and loving you and your body is
    weakened and strengthened,
Making you calm and satisfied. Making your ecstasy and
    "uncommon norm".
The climax that has journeyed you, the sensations that
    have mothered you,
The watery eyelids that testify your manifestation hold
    as testament of triumph.
You love me with your soul.
I am Proud to touch, kiss, dream, and desire.
I am Proud to love you, knowing that your soul is pure
    and complete with me.
Thank you for loving me. We are one.

Date: March 25, 1999

UNREVEALED

With all that is with in me, and all of the love I hold,
Nothing could measure, so it remains untold.

This one page of sweet lullaby, may say a touch of how I truly feel,
Even without words, just a look or caress, my expression of love
seems so unreal.

Somehow I want to share with you, just where I'm coming from.
But only God can relate because of the love he has for us, and his
son.

Unconditional would be the direct meaning of this kind of love,
This, only being given, from the man above.

Since I can't make verbal or written what you mean to me.
The only way to show you is to love you physically.

So, I'll hold you close and treat you right,
Build on our friendship and share insight.

Well, it's about time to wrap it up
But as I stated before,
These true feelings
are what I've longed for.

Intimacy, at this time, does not play a part,
In the depth of the love held with in my heart.

With you, I can laugh and cry,
I am free to be me and with an exhaled sigh,

I thank you for all the love I have learned to know
I thank you for your willingness to grow.

Life on earth, is only experienced one time,
To love, you must have peace to achieve a freed mind.

The Lord has brought me all the joys of life,
And has control of where I stand,

He has brought me you, renewed my strength from a pain filled
soul,
And agreed to take us hand in hand.

With this confidence of being so sure,
It is evident that this relationship will begin pure.

So, to put an end to my struggle to bring my feelings out,
Or at least try,
I'll just say that without a doubt,
I know a love that money cannot buy.

Love Always,

Date: August 28, 1997

SWIMMIN'

Holding my breath
to feel like home–
My mother's womb–
And underwater or inside with you–
I remember.
Closing my eyes
to clench my soul
'cause ecstasy's got me in dreams revisited–
And the touch of skin is
A massage or message
of the eternal tears of joy
that I scream–
Every time we swim–
Go swimmin'
Hips go around
and inside out–
synchronized by our tears flow–
creations of rivers from one extreme
to the valley of streams
that tear down the walls of
contractions
And distractions–
You got me–
We got we
Open
Embracing one only to melt through to
the core of my souls move—ments.
And we move with grace
And we touch with lips to express gratitude.–
We stand in honor and I am honored
to swim with you.

Summer 99'

BREATHE

Inside out and outside in
mesmerized by clouds
reigning down on our heaven-
tongues connecting in whirlwinds
of sensations and heat-
avoiding contact with my souls eyes
I remain in a distant land—daze-
fire struck; earth ablaze—remembering what was-
embracing what awaits.
My foretold future story
lies in the apple of your eye-
You are beautiful—mane of a lion—heart of it's own-
roaring righteously for trespasses of it's dismembered home-
screaming a lion's powerful scream of strength
to resolve the mental confusion and conclusions of life-

not a day in the search did you find
the queen roaring loud—profound-
it seemed—unavoidable
connections between something great
in my fashion—lion disassembling false idols to convert those lost-
I'd never leave the side of my King-
Together fearless and destructive—mounting walls,
breaking down mountains—Lead by an energy,
a force more triumphant than our existence./
Inside out and outside in,
clouds reigning down on our heaven-
and every time we breathe
sea breezes of spiritual excellence moves

our bodies and whispers—soft whispers
speak as a narrative over our motions—MMM!

What a sweet embrace—silent whispers narrate
the depth of a love in it's manifestation-
circular movements—repetitive rotations—notions of freedom-
love unconditional love—Love in it's manifestation-
I don't know what I'll do if I touch you-
      together we'll breathe

April 30, 1999

HOME

As you release the beautiful essence of my fertilization—streams of "Thank God all Mighty" and "I never cried before" cum—down water falls are sea lions roaring and sea horses galloping to freedom. My climax is overwhelmed by your resistance—sprouting up like fertile seeds—we meet our bodies clench and elevate to higher levels of ecstasy leaving us with breath filled MOANS, and tears of births and rebirths and foundation and development-

Consciously aware of our ecstasy driven passions and embraces we admire a deeper soldier—Yes, even deeper than the intangible seed your soul is delivering me right now—People say I should wear a ball and chain but, I AM FREE—bound in freedom my slavery doesn't exist—Planets we orbit—outer space is our meeting place when I can't touch you in the physical—and we rejoice in the mental.

Matrimony hasn't consumed us—we've consumed it—utilizing every moment for growth—Romancin' and makin' love all day in the spiritual—Makin' love all night in the natural—At this moment words run through my head until SSSS! My God—No y'all don't understand I am really callin' him-

Everything deleted history in progress—Manifested beautiful beginnings and your movements have made my cerebral mute—brain dead I am held in a physical acceptance of whispering your name and screaming My My My's and have mercies and reciting poems—singing choruses to songs we dance with no music—recovering from my multiple climax sensations of relaxation and freedom take me-

Exhausted from pleasures our mind and soul embraced—unifying into but one joy—Lying there in puddles of the fruit of our labor we share silences that protest I love you—I need you—I'm yours—You are mine. We are united—Eyes stuck together

I gave up—I'm out for the count—sensing your gaze as I smile—You watch me sleep and I sleep so peaceful knowing that you are holding me—Your eyes close and you reach inside of me to connect our spirits as one–

Side by side our flesh has retained memories and our dreams reflect— through fields and pickin' flowers holding hands through the sun we roam to observe a light that makes the SUN'S RAYS dem—Invited to a place of a new awakening we accept intertwined we ascend—we are love born—again and again, we are home./

May 12, 1999

WALKIN...

The love that I have for you requires no reservations—makes tears happy to make puddles for us to bathe in/ This love beyond satisfaction—touches wholeness and explores—goes beyond what is complete to apply more/ This love, the love I have for you is the direct reflection of your worth—agape and bliss/ together like God and Djembe's talkin' up sons/ The love I have for you makes possibilities endless—keeps me woke at night,/ My night light has contained every last one—I wouldn't let em' leave the room/ If I give you everything but receive nothing I'll die. I want to precipitate with you and make strips of Lavender in Navy skies./ I cogitate on the way you make me feel—and it's reflection—See, I feel blessed to even feel this—Been studying you loving you deeply—But, I can't hold on if you don't even want to be free—If you did, you'd know to just do it. I am your Maxine Waters, flowing through everything to see and protect you. I am your Sojourner, 6'6 when you need me to. I am your food supply, fertile ground, and anointed vessel of armor. I am fly Betty, Aunt Jemma ma sweet like syrup and honey suckle on summer's first day. I am the 1rst constellation you've ever seen walking. I inhibit stars/ Don't sleep I am strong enough to walk away, loving you.

February 15, 2001

BREATHTAKEN

Words spoken with the imagination of a deity
You free me with your speech-
it captivates;
every part of my being

like soft rain-

d
  r
    o
      p
      p
        i
         n
          g
over
    sugar

I melt

My mist exists in the very inflection of your voice-

I am yours for the moments when you take a realm and make it
yours- stepping in with gentle footsteps, I invade your space.

I am submerged in this moment- like baptism
I am dying to be reborn,

held in the water that lives
flowing smooth as river I crossed in ancient wilderness
to provide serene greetings through spirits of ancestors

who lived by flesh once.

I am in this now-

I cannot turn back!

I cannot be bound.

I am free to breathe after the poem, cause you take my breath away.

Thank you.

Ressurrection Graves
August 16th, 2003
Dedication: Ray

POLARIS

Your voice enters my pores like the needles used for past wars-

bringing the sounds of music to one accord-

made whole—made new-

cleansing impurities and overexposed pain-

finding refuge in your being, I AM FREE-

magnetic forces mold our souls into but one host-

hearts resounding into but one beat

and sprits into but one breath-

God has sprinkled his joy into the bodies of masterminds-

we come inside and out of each other's souls to perfect what was and is
to come-

Together in a bond—we dwell—residing in a place-
a time—a conquest of change—cosmic movements—slow—soft—like
the earth's rotation—intertwined by a melodic harmony—we turn to the
sound of the breeze
massaging the surface of your locs
simultaneously my lips touch the melting pot of your soul and your eyes
close as we dance—as we dream—as we meditate—dancing to a
legacy—Righteous beginnings—and my eyes could not resist a moment of freedom—clenched realizing that no moon, no star, no sunset
could reflect this depth of beauty—You speak to me—You touch me—

we dance—my soul embraces and my mind enters this cloud of symphonies—Your into me like my being needs you—Sweet as the smell of pomegranates—kind and understanding—inspirational and collected—like the message in footprint, does our love complete me knowing that if I fall you will carry me—I could use metaphorical visions and universal "norms" to express what has generated the constant building of liquid life circulating to the core of my heart but the battle of simplicity and complexity overwhelm my cerebral functions leaving me speechless—melancholy—distant yet inside—meditating on the ooh's in what you do to me—Mentally, physically, emotionally—healed—exalted—touched; words scramble like the soul train message board—contemplating this state of being I understand.

We inspire—motivate and create safe haven for a soul deemed our own–
Cultivated by a spirit—presence—it's you–
I woke up the next day inside of you only to find comfort in this state of being–
The battle of simplicity and complexity ceased—and the universal norm " I love you" is resistant to vocal essences–

Complexity takes you and me—describes our attributes relative to each other's soul–
I woke up the next day inside of you only to find these words–

In efforts of simplicity,
you are the mate of my soul–

April 30, 1999

BOOK THREE

Evolution of a Lyricist

CHAPTER ONE: NEWNESS

NEWNESS

I saw you last night/ I was walking in the park/ you dispatched the angels to bring streetlights to dark spaces/ filled me up inside, many places that I praise you—no one can fade you, no one can fade you/

You went to hell for us—snatched the keys/ now I live eternally/ I die daily to be washed of the turmoil that I made/ knowing that the righteous lives, I have gained life/ I am not fearful of taking in your light/

I measured your greatness by things of this life—I chose roads that followed pilots of dissension—not to mention/ I have penetrated weakness and made death feel welcome—and now my pains are far less than seldom/

Yo, by grace I live/ by grace I can give and my opportunities for failure have withered—a new seed has been de-livered-planted and saved souls are my mission/ being covenant with him—and spirit filled within/ I am not fearful of the light that blinds—for, my all has poured in to the pro-gress-ion of my third eye/

2nd Verse

Now the newness has set in and new life
is inside—I exalt you beyond, you are
holy and magnified/ I am released from
the world officially gentrified—your
people, peculiar by spiritual definition—this fire in me was not conceived
by man's achievement/
It was out of my expectation that is why
you show us part—for to consume it all
at once would burst a human heart/

The measures by which you brought me
back in—gave me the victory by 2nd chance-
Lord your light in me is completion/
skies they danced wit me like David in
imagery and we rejoiced forever—my
strength is renewed—the bonds of peace
are settled—I am a vessel, Ressurrection
risen to exude/ your beauty—I am a Soul-
Ja by the living water flowing through
me/

You gave me new life and you made everything,
You gave me new life, and you made everything alright.

Come home to me

Come home to me
don't wait and see,
who's right or wrong
come home to me.

Win or lose this fight,
I just want peace
please come home,
come home to me.

It seems like time has passed us by and
made its own way through my life but,
I know there's a chance to have you once
again-
I promise I will cherish each moment.

For so long I've wanted to know you,
but you've taken yourself away from me-
and I am a part of you—I can't help but
love you and
I know you'd love me too—if you . . . .

My life incomplete without you in me,
I am bound, I am not free.
For with you I have gifts, gifts to
receive-
I need you please to forgive me (Lord)
I really want you to consume me
so please come home

October 13–2002

MY TURN

When is it my turn
to feel and not take it back?

When is it my turn
to hold a vow and never give it back?

When can I stand before God?
and all of the angels above
and promise my heart
that is full of love.

I want a turn . . .

Verse 1:

So many Mister Rights but,
somehow it's wrong.
So many lonely nights
but the faith is strong.

So many mistakes made by me,
so many times, I wanted to believe,
that my heaven on earth was around
the corner there waiting just for me.

Repeat chorus:

Poem–

I want a turn to wake up with morning on my lips—glossy without it
costing me my sane—got pain from deep when I think of those moments alone, when alone is too silent/ when I want our eyes to meet—

engage. We'll tell stories like jahle's and we'll do more than drop knowledge, we'll drop wisdom.

I want a turn to feel his love without being rejected—after being infected with the virus of possibility—"It's you and me baby". You know the game—everybody plays cause people residually follow cycles and oppressive habits before stepping out as an individual-ly I be one in a million women who are average-ly above. I stand out because I go beyond the mathematics—I possess the dove/ and though I have imperfection—I am guided. I have never seen love like me – I am love in 360'—I love so much cause I know what it took to love me-

I know the Lord loves me—but the other; he is still out there. I am serving God but all eyes are open—I was made to be a married virtuous woman, for real. It doesn't appeal to those who prefer to keep himself like Paul, but I must share. I got it coming out of my pores.

The arguments vary—You're too young, you're not ready. I wish the excuses would stop sweatin' me—they scared I might catch what I'm fishin' for, or get more. I know the manifestation of God is light rain over me right now, to him. But it's gushy like a river coming through the clouds to bless me—create in me what he needs to fulfill his plan—so I try to stay out of my own hands while he pours and I receive and somebody's response is, "Yeah, but I got needs." I know he met em' but the everyday warfare has got me staring through the skies at em' wondering when is it my turn to become beautifully wifed—we'll merge our position with Christ and change and build and live this life without walking dead—You want us married? How do we distinguish—is there a perfect hookup? That's like trying to figure out whether Alley Mcbeal is Bulimic, or whether Isaac ever got seasick. I want a turn. Turn, turn, turn . . . . I want a turn to be a living testimony a witness to the results of holding fast to the vision—a turn to move the mountains when I witness while tears of joy rain in sacrifice as they listen. And I keep hearing hold fast to the vision . . . . God makes the provision . . . Hold fast to the vision . . . . God makes good decisions though he won't violate our will . . . Hold fast to the vision he has good intentions . . . he makes the provision . . .

just wanna make sure I wait and not take it upon myself to idolize the perfect mate and mission to find him—then become disappointed because his is human and I see flaws. I wanna make sure I do this in the way that God would have the —cause—it would be a shame if I was built up and settled for less than what God would give me—and consider me whining for a minute but my entire being is in it, trying to find the content place that would keep me in welcome place with the holy spirit. I want a turn.

February 17, 2003

MISS U

I miss him so much
How can I miss him like I do-
What I'm saying in my heart
Is that I really miss you/
I miss em' so much how can
one deny this love inside--
I only miss him because I let
him take your place in my life/

When it started, it was so clear, that
this was right.
I took my feelings
let them replace light. /
And now it's not going
the way that I planned
for it to go,
My heart is empty, he didn't replace you-
I became a burdened soul. /

I miss him so much
How can I miss him like I do-
What I'm saying in my heart
Is that I really miss you/
I miss him—so much how can
one deny this love inside--
I only miss him—because I let
him take your place in my life/

When it started, it was so clear, that
this was right.
I took my feelings
let them replace light. /

And now it's not going
the way that I planned
for it to go,
My heart is empty, she didn't replace you—
I became a burdened soul. /

And now the days go on
I persist with sadness in my arms
Hard to breathe but, I press on—

Cause without you I have no pulse
The God that is more than enough. /
(Ensemble sings)
Chorus: x2

End: (Together) I only miss you because, I let him take your place in
my life. /
Speak: Take me back Lord

August 3, 2001

THINKIN' ABOUT YOU

I just keep thinking about you
one day that you'll come home
I just keep thinkin' about you
someday that you will know

I just keep thinkin' about u
won't u come over here
I just keep thinkin about you
but the other side has your peers

I just keep thinkin' about u
but you don't wanna see
that when I'm thinkin' about you
I'm all you really need

So I'll be thinkin' about you
till the cows part the sea
and I'll be thinkin' about you
till you come on home to me.

The life It seems so grand
no responsibilities
you can party when you can
nobody is watching over thee

and the occasional drink
may be what you need

when the stress of life
oversees your abilities

and when you abandon what I have already given thee
I will hold for awhile until you come back to me.

But what If I claim this earth
come back right now,
will you be ready to forgive those
that you daily frown.

will you fear your emotions getting high
because you have lied to yourself all of this time

Do you think I will take you back even though
you chose to leave, what you reap you will sew.

-Ressurrection Graves
March 10, 2002

PERSONAL TIME

I have found a way to live on—
pass the dawning of revelation's born/
I have found a way to rest—
and continue on pass all the mess/

I have found an outlet—
where my heart is free of scorn/
ensemble:
I have found

a new place and nobody's there—
ensemble:
but, I am not alone/
I have found in my heart where tears water,
like flowers bloom in spring—

I have found the pit where my voice comes from
and it's in the joy that my master brings
I have found my destiny—
the one that everybody hopes and dreams for—
the one that everybody searches for to found out
what their life means/
said I have found my destiny and it is the same for you and me/
that I should serve my Lord God with everything
and all things shall be added unto thee./
Oh Lord I thank you, I'm so happy

I have found a place where I belong—
I have found someone to love my whole life long/

And it's deep within my soul–

I have found the man to make me whole.
And the promise is that everything shall be added unto me./

No worries, No complaints, No fears
I have found a place for me, where nobody else exists.

In my personal
time with you Lord, I am truly blessed./
In my Personal time with you Lord,
I am truly Blessed

Early 2002 (March-ish)

MY BAG

At first, my choices were vain
like calling you-
having arguments over time.

like wanting you-
even though I knew, you weren't mine

like stopping by
unannounced.
when fornication didn't
make us pronounced.

I take the bag

Met this young girl who had a baby,
had seen the evidence of her own.
Father
knew who he was-
but he still left them alone.
and she said,
I take the bag

Who ever said we were supposed to know—inside
and how come, my heart just did not realize
I knew this wasn't what I wanted, never was the way I dreamed/
I knew this wasn't what God had for me/
I took a chance at the sweetest hope
It wasn't about the man; it was the fact that he woke
to bring me joy. But, his hurt was so,

I became bruised for the price of being whole.
I did not understand it has never been so bad before,
and even I, in the past have fell short
I saw myself so clear as day, even though now, I am not that
way.
I saw through the eyes of a mad man scorned, the difference is
that I've been reborn
I made a mistake that could've cost me everything
for the hope of love, I endured the pain
Battered, Your worth is exactly the worth of God-
The latter is greater than the surface-
and if it makes you happy—give me the bag and I'll give it to
my pappy
I'll take the bag—don't wanna hold you down (hold down)
I take the bag

I take the bag

for letting you in,
for the whole situation,
for my weaknesses
for my greediness
for taking your power and pretending I did it
for my lame excuses, and my sight without vision
for because your word said you'd forgive me,
I'll take the bag. (hold bag)

BLOOD IS THICKER

Now that I have you,
and now that you are here.
Now that I can see you in me,
and now that I know who's I am.

Please stay close, I need you to stay on me.

When life it tries to woo woo woo me, with
the cares of the world-
just be there Jesus to remind me-
that I am yours,

and when the peace in me struggles to have peace,
please just remind my soul that it's you I'm livin' for.

And to the streets, they try to pave my roads-
Lord, give me the strength to step out and unload . . . . .

I want your glory, to reign in me the same way,
your glory reigns in Heaven now.

Now that I have given you full control,
now that I pray my will is yours, I am whole.

So don't let me do it—no,no,no
don't let me fail, don't let me strain
what I've come so far to share.

So, Don't let me do it.-
I've come this far for a purpose
I know I am special I was purchased,
by the blood of the lamb.

Keep me in your arms
hold me and don't let me go.
In times when I feel alone,
fill me up with your Holy Ghost.

and, Don't let me do it.-
I've come this far for a purpose
I know I am special I was purchased,

by the blood of the lamb.

There are times when I go against your love-
what was set for me, for us/
and my heels become sore, walking is too much.

I want to end this race, to see my triumph.

But if I give up now, I'll never see exactly how,
I made it through, I want to live as you do.

with eternal light in view . . . . .

It hurts me so when I doubt your will
and sometimes I don't even know that I am in fear (repeat)

SO . . . .

Keep me in your arms
hold me and don't let me go.
In times when I feel alone,

fill me up with your Holy Ghost.

and, Don't let me do it.-
I've come this far for a purpose
I know I am special I was purchased,
by the blood of the lamb.

The blood/ is thicker than the water is my skin./
The blood/ is more than the blood within my veins./

The blood is the joy of my soul
is what makes me whole is the blood of the slain.

The blood shed just for me,
cleansed so that I can breathe

This blood-
is the blood shed for me,
that the righteous shall be,

Oh—the blood of the lamb.

The blood of the lamb

The blood of the lamb .
lamb
straight, no movement
lamb

-Ressurretion Graves 2001
typed in: February 23, 2002

LET GOD

I wish I had all the answers contained in a bag, so you could pick and choose those things, that would make your heart glad./

Iwish I had this big bag, used for dumping dead works—so that you could come and fill it up with the things that made your heart hurt.

I know that I'm not just human and because he lives in me, It seems like I am him to you But, I am still changing.

And I would love to be the one to supply you every need, as a friend I love you, but I can make you complete.

Let Go Let God help you
Let Go Let God fix it for you–
For the rain like your tears, falls and changes it evaporates to rain again.
But the joy of it all, is that when it falls, when it falls . . . .

Let Go, Let God fix it for you–
Iwill always be your friend, and though until the end–
Iwill pray with you see you through and I love you once again,
but, even friends, I can't make you live again.

Ressurrection Graves
July 2001

PSALM 23:5

I know sometimes you want people to love you
and time more often than not, they will hate.

They are haters.

But there's a place in God's heart that each song represents
and you are blessed, and they will see you surpass their efforts.
because ...

He's prepared a place for me,
more than just a plate to eat.
Included is the table in front of thine enemies.
repeat one time

Always remember that
our strength is above ourselves—
we get burnt out
but, God always shares.

so when they want to talk about your pain.
when they want to dog your name,
when they choose to hate instead of pray,
that baby is when you change!

when you think it's over and it's just begun.
when your suicide notes are left for someone,
when your failures for God make you too ashamed

to pray, cause somebody said that you can't,
that baby is when you change!,
and say,

and what he's prepared, know one can take away, but you.
no one change the love between God and you, no one can take away,
but you.
only you can change the way you move, and no one can take away,
not even hate, cause you're protected by mercy and grace, no one can
take it away. No body, no human, can take something super natural away.
once you believe—it's activated and true—it's been tried before you, no
one can take it away.

January 2002

BATTLES WITH THE DEFINITION OF GOD!

When stomach vessels get queasy and acid lining becomes passionate toward

inner skeletons, I hear anthems of acrobatic measurements making love to ear

drums in soft conditions—Bliss owned mystics warn me about the fishes in deep

sea waters with no scuba gear—divers in thoughts that sustain depth to quench

salt water and abstain death/ requests of immortality beyond corned

convenience, soakin' religious toe nails in unrighteous pas-story, I got a

penetration grievance/ Ordained regurgitation by militant anger— thirsting

for repossession of cultural significance inhaling smoked incense—soaked in

puddles of wine/ redemption without focal inscription you get holy spir- ited by

publicized devil baptism/ while he laughs at the ignorance of men in shortages, when extended first and foremost—grand audiences toast the most by

quality applaud—Battles with the Definition of God/

October 2000

HOLOCAUST

Just did it completed the whole album now I'm finished/
Time to tour—take my daughter/ give shout outs to the Lord/
I'm floored—a connoisseur of Joy-
Strictly captured—eternal satisfactory/

My locks permeate the son—my heart is ablaze-
Makes me dance Ancient African laced Amazing grace/
I faced tragedies hard to bear some would testify—from side-
    lines/
They remained—scared; I said, "Dare you—I come prepared!"
Take my weapon to hold me down,
As I enter battleground/
I clench my fist and rock the plow-
Soldiers cut my grass to weed the dead works out/
Hate is wak/ grab the chorus and spit it out/

Chorus:
We can do it like the holocaust
I pray that everybody dies to self-
Massacres of Resurrections—feelin's felt-
spirits strip the block-
got no time to hear the ticking of the judgment clock.

Rode on the backs of bucks trained to attack
Those who step and try to make contact/
Deliverance I experience by whispers of his name-
I bleed him—I need him—let my seeds swim in his veins/
freed them to equate the information—salvation; releasing the
    old of ways-

brighter days exist—if you feel this turn to your neighbor—in
reverence, submit love through pounds—exhaust how/

I have never arrived and never will—I will learn until dusk is the
remnants of his will for me/ Stand as freedom makes new
seams for me/ and the anthems of my music rests in the con-
crete of barren streets/block gatherings—police matters
fathomless/ break the jails down—engage in love that sur-
passes sound—move the mount and exude the resurrection
by living to tell the story—The jahle are the evidence of his
glory/

I wanna bring it funky yo'—so you can hear me spit it—the words
evaporate in brown soil to grow trees of life within it/ And, I
am a lyricist by trade-mark if anything—spoken word is my
heart; my art/ Got fossils dancing to the rhythm—request-
ing this song all over existence/ underground; dust becomes
life after this/ beat we meet the lyrics and rock the dj's
booth—methods of becoming new/
Take a situation given—refer to 16: 9 2 Chronicles—King James
Version, Chapter 5/ check 11; read it aloud for you and I—
cause dust returns like measures in time/

And though I die, I'm thankful my chance was extended-
Pray so loud Lucifer flees to release the tension/
God himself should get a pension—for presiding in me-
A holocaust might really set the captive free/

Clap your hands to da beat-
Grand ladies, tap yo' feet/
Young folks get out cho seat-
Everybody hit the chorus 2 da beat!

-Ressurrection Graves 8/2/01 completed

BOOK FOUR

"When I say Resur–You say rection, Resur-rection, Resurrection!"

CHAPTER ONE: I AM RESSURRECTION

I AM RESSURRECTION
(SLAM VERSION)

I am Ressurrection, not the Resurrection, the Resurrector—just me.

I come without form or fashion just absent from the body to exchange pain, with Joy. Some can't get used to the new name cause they think they know me—That blows me/Ressurrection is everything that I have ever been in God's calculated form—forgiven—and risen—I come back from the graves-

Just to keep the microphone warm—for you/

I stand before you nakedly and risk being called anything—less than—not worthy of/

I ain't here to pretend to be prophetic—I am graced—blessed with holy boldness and I stand clearly in his image—like I would Michael Jordan at a Wizards scrimmage—Blemished,

Blemished and torn where my life had broken standards and boundaries were not set so I increased my failures—and you wonder why he gave me—Ressurrection the Spiritual Soul-Ja.

I can make lists of times that I was not acting like a Christian—But, that is why I am forgiven. Your love might help me see evidence of the son in sweet rotation—help me make differences where my boundaries exist risk taken—God is so patient—Days numbered like I notice when rays of the son seem missing—some days I just thank him because I am living-

Everybody relates to pain—I want an audience who can relate to change—Forget the marketing and the rented Bentley to impress you—I came in my Suzuki Esteem to testify that my God reigns and loves you no matter what you do./

and Ressurrection has weathered storms—all while God kept me

warm in his word—Ver-ba-tum I apply it to safe stages like—my shower—praise him for hours/ water sort of had me frozen when I finished-
I have been chosen wit lips scented; frankincense did it-
had you paralyzed from the waste down-
cause I am intoxicating from the inside and on the way out/
Stronger than coffee black I attack situations with forces
distort your fond memories with light exposure/ Spiritual Soul-Ja present to hold it down—in spite of the haters I will advance from stagnate grounds/ Ignition of the pen to cum all over the paper, left the after party of the performance so you can soak it in later/
I elevate from my adolescence to the woman I am—been struggling not to throw the hands—cause it's just easier sometimes-
we rely on the methods that require little thought—so in situations now I pray stronger—so not to offend anyone's face with my fist—heavy like ten forklifts-
I am Ressurrection, not the Resurrection, the Resurrector—just me.
I come without form or fashion just absent from the body to exchange pain, with Joy. Some can't get used to the new name cause they think they know me—That blows me/Resurrection is everything that I have ever been in God's calculated form—forgiven— and risen—I come back from the graves—Just to keep the microphone warm—for you/
For real—I just want what God has in store, I owe it to him—for the incredible distribution of grace—On time—never ceasing to infiltrate the situation and make improvements/ handle all my loose ends/
I am Ressurrection, not the Resurrection, the Resurrector—just me.
I come without form or fashion just absent from the body to exchange pain, with Joy. Some can't get used to the new name cause they think they know me—That blows me/Resurrection is everything that I have ever been in God's calculated form—forgiven— and risen—I come back from the graves—Just to keep the microphone warm—for you/

POETRY MANIFEST

My poetry's too deep for me to feel right now-
Pray that my senses come back to present day Adventist like
7 days to worship seems like life lines apart/ 'cause love settles in
my art/
Formatin' around the curves in my arch/ the letters they are blurs/
My insides rot/ vexation in a D-flat form where the basis remains
that I can't relate to my own art form/ 'cause it's too deep and
I'm at the shallow end of consciousness, dealin' wit—higher levels
of bullsh**/ like—should I wake up in the morning and fornicating
got me questioning whether I should be hoeing to get this love
behind me/ that tortures my insides and some how blind me/
Now thought about getting a ring in my brow to keep the lids
open—but my soul is vulnerable to present day Adventist like 7
days working hard to glorify the apprentice of my existence/ goes
this master-piece from which I write—Been freestylin' for weeks.—
tight poems and lyrics that creep creepin' from inna to the outta
man to the skies—Most often I submit prayers that soothes the
stars and massages their minds.-
My illness keeps me in this realm and often times the sickness of
my spittage masturbates on my brain seals/ cells like bondage/
slavery I am in—I can't understand the thoughts of my insides
even though I'm the Poet. / Just flowin' 'cause the energy is letting me freestyle like dreadlocks and Corporate suits—Hungry
consistently to avoid destruction; My words bring healing and
light but, I am suctioned/ soaked into by the memories and the
yesterdays of when a man loves a woman dances/ without the
proposal of second chances and glances become reactions to
what's deep down—and sometimes when I look at the star that
navigates—I feel home somehow/ 'cause I could stare at your

beauty til' you transcended the light and gave me a little to say
"Hey, Mista", who's the leader and the light—Missing you has got
me lifeless/ makin' love to my Winnie the Pooh night lights/pillows
become like carousels/ they rotate the energy by warmth alone/
And, times I wish you'd come home/ like your spirit is a piece 'cause
a breath taken from you is a life murderin' me; over tea./ Miscella-
neous, anonymous, out of circuits like old friends that resurface/
we over and I've telepathically orbited in your soul—is where I
rest my head./ Compounded these anthologies and dissertations
that plays through our head—Pause—Skip that message;/ I'm
feelin' it coming back again—It was the moment/ but it existed/
that means it's still hope-less-ly, hope—that is less likely to become failure/ like death/ 'cause I am Ressurrection/ Breathe so I
can have life again/ staggering by weakness—you genius—
breathing life in men/.

Let me inhale and taste existences of immortal breath. / Ascend
with me—dream or fantasize so that I can have one last dance
with your chest/ on my face—face on your chest/ Fingertips
speak like conquests-

When you breathe, I am the living; by spirit I exist/Lord only you
can control the true life in this bliss/-

Date: July 25, 2000

ANKH TREE

(Poetry Manifest Returns . . .)

Bliss and you did Lord-
Handle your business/Brought light through the North Star to
visit my spirit on a humble/ submission to flesh made us fumble a
few times but I wrote this rhyme to remember how I got blessed—
You brought me certified and signed by God's omnipotence; dili-
gence/—his patience to exist in me without the Freedom of a
submissive being. See I road the road blind without seeing; believ-
ing the way faith intended, I try and I breed—multiply my young
I be the Ankh Tree/ Apprehended I remember how the love began—a kiss sparked an eternal incision that would pierce
backwashed skin/ a jack-knife caused me to scream—Present
agony remains in the distance between—air like time./ Most
people want to rock ice to show ends—(pause) I just want to be
rockin' him/ on fingers, toes, my movements like degrees—and in
times when I'm tired he could breathe through me/ Now that's
one, spirit—chastening righteousness I do agree—this man ain't
God, but he planted seeds/ that would grow based on my soil,
cast down dead weeds to rise from sinnin'—rooted in blood I boil
in it/ I feel the Ankh Tree risin' while I spit it./ Fit into brain cau-
tions—love in true identity, you can see the tip of the plant
exploding out of me/ dread head girl—I be the one with the locs
— I be the enigmatical underground—I be hip-hop, flavor/ Spit-
u-ally, I be the Ankh tree by all possession—let my wings muster
you with whispers—soft whispers like the world as my hips talk-
conversatin' after a night out at the juke joint/ this, this thing is
beyond stalkin' me it's become my oxygen—the way that I am
stimulated/ reflective lenses pacify my internal masturbations/
he be massagin' me when I'm just thinkin' about gettin' some/
Yo, King I love God more than your throne—as long as he walks
through you, your invitation is always home/ So, to the seas that
turn red if we just put our tips in it—to the days that lie ahead

when we sample Egypt and feel the ancestors through spirit/ toe
touches purify it; cleans my sins and draws vibrations—climax
driven; Languished in this venue I feed the need that nurtures
me; grows in me . . .
This possession be the Ankh in me-
I be the Ankh tree/

Ressurrection the Spiritual Soul-Ja
Completed: August 23rd, 2000

NECESSARY

Why is it that I bask in you?
Fast in you/
Head wrapped; Bushed-
I suck the sap from the nectar of your skin; Barks
Sparks of happiness glisten to reminiscent scents of you/
I, from the very roots where you started feed.
Grown from being devoured from broken hearted—I bleed,
Miseries out to intake gladness/
We when together extol the existence of being one, hold residence in
the vibration of the son; birthed to save us-
completely submerged, I purge in you/
Glow profusely to reflect us in a light that God would organize—me
with you/ With God as central, his will fulfilled.

You capture me.

Tasteless even—Just Heaven—the sensation/
I feel you when I'm in motion-
Find u necessary to be lifted-
(EXIT SPLIFF FROM MY EXISTANCE)
My high can only be attained by God by me—by you-
By us; by we be necessary-
Scriptures become memory as we—study for improvement/
By hearing and hearing we are changed.-
Become centered by quotes and prayers like "In Jesus name".

I bask in you-
Fast in you.
I must confess we cried as a conversation to share juices—turned com-

bustion into mineral roots-n-soil/
Made it wet to generate the execution of increase—yes created the
oxygen that we now breathe; trees innate—we, created, to become one—
made mistakes along the way but the journey molded our paths of righteousness back—determined to give it all we've got-
peace for one!
You are necessary to remind me of blessings-

Irefuse to exist useless—of you-
You are necessary for me/

Give thanks for cause and effect—breathed and bled rhythm/ Freedom to co-exist such complete bliss-

Cause life is without it's ecstasy
if my steps are beating pavement without you.

Effect: something would always seem missing, my pores would not per-
spire the same—I would not journey the same path/

With you my tears become puddles for us to bathe in together—for
Joy-
Pleasures would never be whole without what is necessary like flesh
and water. Sort of . . . but deeper.

A dosage of you would heal me—not sustain or remiss
My condition-

Your spirit is necessary so we can taste spaces between each other,
Measure the distance and move beings to over stand—Place us in
atmospheres to allow us this measure-
Komplexed, simply stated,
Necessary
Forever.

August 8, 2001

DROPPIN' OF THE BAGS

(Poem goes with the song My Bag)

Now 6 years since conception
moving toward the climax of adolescence,
Faith has told Hope they should believe cause
too many has lost the strength to
and I, I stand at the edge of everything
to approach heaven correctly—cause most things
are directed by our figures and assumptions-
many of us divide and measure the consistency in which to
believe length wise like multiple children during tax season-
everybody got a reason to reside hopeless and show promi-
nent states
of Bliss outside one's self –wit—red eyes and slow tenden-
cies-

I can't imagine that feeling like freedom-

So yes, I will take the baggage for the dirt that I dug, specifi-
cally the shadow that
formed my Graves but, as you can see Ressurrection is the
evidence that Jesus saves I believe and-

This brother would hold me at night—didn't know he was
present cause I didn't
invite him—he consumed the dreams that made me uneasy—
I woke up wit regrets cause
it was difficult to shake the disease of Hatred—but, that could
be fatal like my Lips in a Poetry slam make opponents wish
they could be apart of the Matrix, to control me—wish they

could twist my lips like an African and put bones in it to dedicate to the Egyptians and I would still rip it-

Just like an Alliance of Runway models featuring thickly figured African women.
And, that brother I was talking about—yeah I told him this in my spirit and somewhere he's got to be hearing it-

I love you.

I wonder whether your skin is still smooth-smooth enough for me to caress it with my softness—flossin' God's awesomeness I got water supplied for your thirst—obey it. I got the devil defeated we can stomp on his head while we create new verses—you like room service just available in my mind-

I have prayed for tomorrow to be new without you but, I gotta wonder if this is bondage or are you somewhere praying to God that I never forget you cause every time I get to the moment before—you return—you return so strong that I could create you if I stare into the midst long enough.

And despite the despair I've caused myself by countless dreams that I recur for self indulgence, I return to dust and form again cast down my imagination that had you paved in it. And Yes, I am tough—but, you break me down inside and I have to go to another dimension and leave you there for weeks at a time, til you consume that world and spill over into my current living-

And despite your absence, you are still a present for me.

Is this bondage I wonder or are you somewhere praying to God that I never forget you.
I am praying to God that he'd release me from you if you are not coming back this time.

Goodbye is getting old—how many times have I officially let you go and now you've run but I can still hear you steps beating against my walls-

It just feels like something is less without you.

But, in this case and most, I know that I am more—don't let the poetry fool you. And sometimes, FEELINGS, are not what's best for you.

And, I take the bag because God said that he'd forgive me and that I would be new and whole again so, I will take our stuff for you, give it to God and stand forgiven. I like to be resurrected, it's among the Gods that I am extended and this poem is about the fact that I will take whatever you give me, but, I ain't gotta keep it.

Ladies we have got to see that our feelings keep us feinin'. And for every moment that we walk out of the spirit, we cheat on God. Then we wonder why we don't have a Husband. If you can't be faithful to God, how you going to be faithful to man-
. I take the bag cause I know how to discard of it. I don't want to carry around my or anyone else's pain for remembrance.

I take the bag for the decisions that have not been best—but Lord rest me—I confess to be imperfect that is why it is in your image that I have been raised-
I do not intend to frustrate your grace for me-

So I take the bag cause I am tired of running from my own shame-
and if you come back right now, I want to be taken
not shaken with fear cause I ignored you-

Unmask me and let me see myself for what truly exists.

Create in me a hatred for my iniquities so that I can be victorious.

Help me to align my will with the will that is God—make my will yours so

that I will, to not oppress myself with the things of this world-

so that I will to not jeopardize my health with sickness cause I need a ground that I can stand on and I need a foundation that the mountains can rock grains on wit my CD-

Free me.

December 2, 2001

Book Cover:
UAN/Desynwerkz
William Flowers
Graphic Design/Web Development
240-988-5621

Photography:
Mindseye Photo & video
Bruce Edwards
editb@comcast.net
www.mindseyephoto.net

Make-up:
Ph.aces of Faith
Make-up Artistry
Letitia Thornhill
703-801-5161

Hair:
Locktician
Disc Hair Design
Camille E. Robbins
301-335-6257

Special thanks to:
Jerilyn Brooks (you know why :-)
and...
Thomas McAteer and the Xlibris Staff
I appreciate your persistence in making sure that this project was well produced. You have been a blessing. Be blessed in your endeavors.

- Ressurrection